I0456343

the OLIVE GROVE

by NARCISSE NAVARRE

THE OLIVE GROVE

Edited by Marzio Ombra & RJ Locksley

Published by Digital Alchemist, LLC

ISBN: 978-09846654-6-4

Printed in the United States of America.

The Olive Grove is dedicated to my wonderful husband,
who encourages my incorrigibly dirty mind.

*"There is a serene and settled majesty to woodland scenery
that enters into the soul and delights and elevates it,
and fills it with noble inclinations."*
–Washington Irving

Giovanna had been named after her grandmother, a woman whose *pasta puttanesca* was said to have ensnared her grandfather Eliseo after just one bite. Her name, long since shortened to Gia, and her predilection for Italian food were the only things truly Italian about her.

As a child, sitting at the dinner table with her sisters, Gia rolled her eyes every time the legendary love story of her grandparents came up. They had met during the olive harvest. He was from Rome and she was from the small hill town of Tivoli–an easy conquest, or so her grandfather thought. *Nonna* Giovanna saw through Eliseo's rambling ways and gave him the run-around for several years. Desperate, Eliseo would stand in the middle of the piazza, guitar in hand, and sing into the late hours of the night, begging for a chance. His voice was so terrible, the story went, that soon the entire neighborhood was pleading with *nonna* Giovanna to marry him just to shut him up.

It wasn't until Gia grew up that she could appreciate their story. Whether it was a tall tale or the truth, no one knew for certain, but it was the kind of feel-good yarn that inspired a wistful sigh.

At nearly thirty, Gia had yet to successfully cook *pasta al dente* or score a relationship that lasted for more than a few months. Striking romantic gold akin to her grandparents was seeming more and more like a fantasy. She whiled away evenings at speed-dating marathons and New Age tantric sex courses for singles. Fifteen accounts on various online dating sites had only yielded a string of men with foot fetishes, mamma's boys or divorcées looking for women half their age. In short, Gia was unlucky.

She had gone to several meditative workshops and had taken up yoga in hopes of unwinding the knot of tension in her belly but nothing had worked. Sex seemed to do the job except Gia despised one-night stands and the awkwardness that followed.

Unlike *nonna*, Gia lacked the olive skin and the raven tresses so prevalent in the Italian side of the family. She wasn't statuesque nor did she take after her mother, whose seductive, hazel eyes could stop a man in his tracks. Gia took after her father, a Brit, whose genetic gifts included hair the color of washed-out wheat and a pale complexion that burned easily. Curvy and slightly plump, Gia was always envious of the lithe and svelte physiques of her fellow New Yorkers. It didn't help that she worked in the fashion industry—a virtual smorgasbord of emaciated women.

Gia had always been curious about her heritage, but the trip to Italy had been an impulsive decision. It was amazing what folly an inbox of screaming clients and years of corporate enslavement could inspire.

In an unaccustomed display of self-assurance, armed with a pitiful Italian vocabulary comprised of *buon giorno, arrivederci* and a handful of colorful curses, Gia booked seven nights in Rome and three in Tivoli. The booking process occupied the whole morning. After maxing out three credit cards, she felt strangely elated, as if a weight had been lifted from her shoulders.

A smirk curled her lips as she mulled over the possibilities. Scenes of hot-blooded Italian men armed with accordions, wild sexual escapades in the dark corners of St. Peter's followed by quick getaways on Vespas elicited an incredulous chuckle. Who was she kidding? If she was lucky, she'd get her ass pinched by some toothless old man in a pizzeria.

In spite of her exhaustive plans, as the day of departure neared, Gia was beset by nerves. Her ten-day trip to Italy might as well have been to the moon. She packed three huge suitcases only to realize she could barely manage one. Finally, she settled on the smallest of the bags and a backpack where she could store essentials in case her luggage was lost. She liked redundancy, security and preparedness and somehow managed to stuff half her medicine cabinet in an already-bulging suitcase.

Before boarding the plane she crossed herself and said a Hail Mary asking *nonna* to watch over her. Sure enough, her overnight flight was uneventful. In fact, the majority of her stay in Rome was uneventful–something she came to resent. Her loose itinerary had unfolded without a hitch. People were friendly and most spoke English. She had no trouble navigating Rome and within a couple of days had settled into a delightful routine: breakfast at the rooftop terrace of Hotel Mozart, a short stroll past the Babuino on her way to the Spanish Steps or a quick left or right on Via Condotti. She hadn't bothered with the metro, choosing to explore the city on foot.

Along the way, she had befriended a few tourists and developed a crush on Valentino, a Vatican Museum guide who ushered her through thousands of years of history in forty-five minutes, but none had offered romantic possibility. While Valentino had doted on her questions, suggestively grazed against her, smiling and flirting, there had been a definite wedding band on his finger. The universe, of late, was proving to have a quite a sense of humor. Valentino! No one that good-looking, named after the god of love, should be married!

The Eternal City offered more than the meager seven days allowed. To compensate, Gia spent days checking off must-see sights from her never-ending list of tourist attractions. In the evening, she returned to the hotel exhausted. It was a good kind of tiredness, the type that beckoned her to a hearty meal in the rooftop terrace followed by curled, peaceful slumber in the cramped coziness of her room. By the fifth day, she had toured the splendors of Trevi, the Pantheon, Navona, the Capitoline, Borghese, the Vatican and even made her way to obscure corners like Caracalla and La Boca della Verita. It was a rigorous schedule that left her very little time for eating, shopping or relaxing.

On the day of departure, Gia was so tired she overslept and missed the first bus to Tivoli. Relegated to the Hotel Lobby for two long hours, she took the time to plan the last three days of her journey. Seventeen miles away, Tivoli was a renowned retreat from the harried life of Rome. Popes and emperors had built fantastic gardens and sprawling villas, all of which wound up on Gia's ambitious agenda. With corporate efficiency, Gia plotted her itinerary, making sure to include savory places to eat and ample time to visit her grandmother's ancestral home.

Tivoli unfolded before her like a dream and the awful, winding traffic leading up to its summit—a nightmare. What should have taken half an hour stretched into a grueling two-hour commute. Contrary to her pep talk, Gia arrived drained. Upon check-in, she settled for a walk around the town, stopping briefly at the house where her grandmother had lived.

The ancestral home was dilapidated and in serious need of attention. A desiccated garden barred by a lopsided gate faced the small piazza where Gia imagined her grandfather had embarrassed himself long ago. The home was still in her family's name but no one had lived in it for a generation. Even the old caretakers had moved on, leaving behind an impersonal real estate agent responsible for running the heat in the winter.

The creaky gate gave way to a short, cobbled path. The stucco had cracked and fallen from the walls. Gripped by sadness, Gia neared the entryway, approaching as one would a shrine. Above her head, a balcony jutted from the masonry—still regal in its decay. A peek through grimy panes revealed the entrails of what was once a happy home, brimming with laughter and love. Gia had come to Italy hoping to find the joy of her heritage but as she looked at the ramshackle remains of her grandmother's home there was no joy—only regret. No one in her family had taken any interest in the home and soon there would be nothing left.

She walked away with a new weight on her shoulders. As the gate closed behind her, Gia knew that she would return. Somehow, some day she would right the wrong. She would find the paperwork and—. The thought was cut short by the impossibility of the task. Gia smiled, taking a look at the home one last time, realizing that she was kidding herself. *Under the Tuscan Sun* was a fiction—people didn't really move across the world on a whim to fix up old houses. Or did they?

The growl in her stomach was the only answer to be had. Gia was useless on an empty stomach. A short walk resulted in a lovely bistro overlooking terraced olive groves and a decent bottle of *Frascati Superiore*. The alcohol muted the loneliness and the thoughts that clamored for attention. Illusions of bathing in fountains, restoring old homes, falling in love and living

La Dolce Vita coalesced splendidly into a dark mood. In the evening, Gia wandered the old town, indulging her blues in the winding, cobbled streets. It was the first time during her trip that Gia had slowed down and she was unsure it was a good idea. The next few days, she vowed, would be decidedly different. She would take her time, linger and enjoy—shake the gloom.

What remained of Hadrian's once pompous villa stretched in all directions. "Where the hell am I?" Gia groused, turning the travel guide upside down in hopes of ascertaining some semblance of direction. To the left and right stretched rows upon rows of ancient olive trees, gnarled and aromatic in the afternoon sun. There were no signs, only half-excavated fragments of Roman walls. Gia threw her hands up, exasperated. "Great, that is just great, Gia!"

Mustering the courage to travel to Italy had been a phenomenal leap of self-confidence but as Gia squinted up at the beaming sun she felt a sudden pang of fear. She was all alone in some distant part of the ruins in the midst of an olive grove with not a single soul in sight. In fact, had she paid closer attention to the lecture about Hadrian, instead of staring at her Roman tour guide's gorgeous lips, she would undoubtedly be more enthusiastic about her current predicament.

Gia was used to the bustle and noise of the city that never slept, not the tranquility of the sprawling countryside. Dotted with ancient ruined palaces, long toppled by hubris and time, the vast olive groves surrounding Tivoli were quiet to a fault. Only the chirping sounds of cicadas and the rustling of the breeze could be heard.

The place was peaceful and she should have felt at ease but the air of decadence that lingered in the grounds unnerved her. It was as if the blood of the slaves that built Hadrian's playground had somehow seeped into the earth, calling her from some unknown place.

Gia loosened the ponytail that held her waist-long hair. Sweat clung to her t-shirt and dripped down her back. Her sandals were caked with the reddish dirt up to her ankles, making her feel even grimier. They were definitely the wrong shoes for exploring the winding dirt paths in the ninety-degree heat.

"It's fine, Gia," she told herself, uncapping a water bottle. "You live in New York City, girl, just breathe." The water was still cool from the last fountain she had refilled at. Gia could have sworn she had been at the ruined baths not ten minutes ago, but couldn't remember which way they were. She had walked in a daze straight into an olive grove, one of many along the three-hundred-acre park.

Don't panic, she thought, recapping the bottle and shoving it back in her bag. "You can do anything, even come to Rome and not have a single guy pinch your ass."

It was late June and the olives were the size of peas. Wiping her forehead with her forearm, Gia stared in awe at the ancient branches. It was always her nature to make the best of terrible situations. There were far worse things in life than being lost in the glory of the Italian countryside, four thousand miles away from her troubles.

Squinting, Gia leaned against the trunk of a tree and checked the time. It was nearly two and already the restaurants would be closing. If she rushed she might find a bar or pizzeria nearby that remained open through siesta but the prospect was daunting. She didn't know the area and with her luck she'd be served whole squids complete with eyes. The thought made her stomach churn. Survivor appetizers were off the menu for the rest of the trip.

Skipping breakfast had not been the brightest idea but neither was coming halfway across the world alone. Gia liked to think that she was being daring and adventurous and that somehow coming to Italy in search of her heritage would change her life but so far she had only felt the intensity of her loneliness.

"Where am I going anyway? What's the hurry?" she said, slinging her backpack down at the base of a gnarled tree. Not like anyone will miss you, she thought somewhat sadly as she took a seat, stretching her legs upon the grass. Gia rummaged through the contents of her backpack and found the sealed pack of trail mix. She had food and water and she was in a beautiful place. It was more than she could say for her spartan apartment back home where she was crammed in with three annoying roommates, two of whom were drama queens constantly at each other's throats.

The sun filtered through the minty green of the grove casting long, diagonal shadows across the wild flowers. A few dots of flaming red poppies intermingled with the purple of dandelion and yellow daisies. It was a pastoral scene worthy of a painting.

Gia sighed, leaning back against the trunk of the tree, chewing the dried raisins and apricots interspersed with salty peanuts. A gentle, cooling breeze rustled the leaves and brought respite from the ferocious heat of the sun. Having had her fill, Gia folded up the bag of trail mix and fanned herself with the guide book. Apparently it was the only thing it was good for. The effort only made her hotter and soon enough she discarded the idea. She tossed it atop her bag and slid out of her sweaty t-shirt, remaining in her undershirt—a silky black lacy thing that could barely pass for a garment.

There was something about expensive, satiny lingerie that made her feel special. Gia skimped on a lot of luxuries and saved her money but it was difficult to resist designer perfumes and undergarments. The idea of wearing something wonderfully ornate and seductive underneath the armor of the corporate suit thrilled her. Most women bought such things for the men in their lives but Gia had long since lost hope of showcasing her vast arsenal of seductive lingerie to the male of the species.

Bunching up the t-shirt into a pillow, Gia rested her head against the tree, allowing herself to shed the sense of fear and embrace her beautiful surroundings. She was about to make good on her vow to slow down and savor the remainder of her stay. She watched idly as the clouds rolled overhead, scattering patches of shadows amidst the grove. Sparrows frolicked, fluttering between the trees, darting to and fro.

The tranquility of the desolate spot and the refreshing breeze lulled her senses. Sleep came slowly, creeping into lids made heavy by the noon-day sun. Within minutes, Gia succumbed to her exhaustion, nodding off peacefully at the base of the tree.

Oviello the Keeper grinned, watching the girl from a distance, emerald eyes roaming along her sunlit curves. He had trailed her for over an hour as she wandered the ruins, waiting for the right opportunity to lure her closer to the veil that obscured his kind from humanity. Oviello knew the dangers of such a breach, knew full well the risks involved in joining with a mortal but, like the rest of his ilk, he was prone to throw caution to the wind.

Slowly, he approached the slumbering girl, his cloven steps silent. He moved with the dexterity of a predator, his muscles rippling beneath sun-bronzed skin. Oviello knelt beside her, his long, black braids streaming forward to tickle her upper arms. He lowered his face to hers and paused, his mouth inches from parted lips. Taking a deep breath, he inhaled hers, fully drinking in the scent of her skin—lavender and rose, sweat, desire. She was salty and spicy, aroused by the wicked dreams he weaved for her.

Shamelessly, he hopped over her, the mahogany fur of his haunches grazing her hips as he squatted over his slumbering prize. The girl's leg was bent, exposing the creamy skin of an inner thigh. The thought of burying himself between her legs stirred him beyond measure. Oviello lowered his hips until the moist tip of his aching erection pressed hotly against her flesh. "Dream of me," he whispered in his ancient tongue, his voice husky and low against her ear. Beneath him the girl shifted, her breaths quickening. "Dream of me," he repeated, more softly, fueling the spell with his scorching lust.

The tiny, desirous gasp that escaped her parted lips thrilled him. Gia's chest rose and fell, the hard tips of her nipples pushing against the sheer fabric. Hair framed her flushed face in a ring of honey-spun gold. Her fluttering eyelids and quickening breaths spoke of dreams.

Satisfied that she was ensorcelled by his spell, Oviello reluctantly eased up. Slipping his powerful arms under her, he stood. She was but a feather in his arms, tiny and precious and all his. With a wicked smile he strode away, carrying his captive deeper into the grove.

Only in certain places did the lands once ruled by Bel meet the mortal world. The site of Hadrian's ancient villa, once a meeting place for his kind and theirs, where the ancient magic was still strong, was one of them. The ancient gods had all but been abolished by the one god–the bleeding man upon the cross of sticks–and since then everything had changed. As man gave up old ways, the children of the laughing god began to fade along with their playgrounds. Oviello's people were but a fading memory, forever relinquished to friezes and statuary, tales and dreams. They were creatures of legend and myth, mere figments of overactive imaginations–or so men thought.

They lived on in scattered pockets where the energy of the land was pure. Only during certain times of the year, during festivals that still secretly venerated their kind, was the veil between worlds thin enough to allow passage. It was during these times that his brothers and sisters took the form of men and women and ventured forth into the vastness of mortal existence for a few days at a time to revel and sow their seed.

Through the ages they had sired many children of Bel's blood, who, in their own unexpected ways, kept the dream alive. The woman in his arms was such a creature, as it would have been impossible for him to spy her otherwise. Oviello had been quietly contemplating his grove when he saw her as clear as day, map in hand, walking in the noon-day sun.

Ducking under a low-lying branch, he wondered whether to tell his brothers of his discovery. They would be furious if he did not share. He gazed down at the beauty in his grasp and smiled. There would be time enough for proper introduction, but he had no intention of sharing her just yet.

Oviello hadn't had the pleasure of a mortal woman in several years. Sure, there were maenads, dryads and nymphs, but their tiresome games wearied him. They preferred mortal men and the price to pay for a good rutting was steep. Furthermore, mating with one of his kind was nearly impossible. They needed the fertile seed and wombs of mortals to continue their species, that or goats and the prospect of a goat was not entirely appealing.

Strong, muscled thighs clambered upwards along the hillside to his home. The thought of mating with a doe turned his stomach. No, with any luck the girl in his arms could serve him and his brothers well, maybe even—. He shook his head. No. He had just poached her from the world of the waking. Oviello would consider himself lucky if she still wanted to mate with him after realizing he'd tricked her into crossing into his world. Perhaps it was best to keep her dormant, he thought, mulling over the situation. With each step his thoughts became more troubled as he crossed the threshold of his home. Would she be horrified?

Two pock-marked columns of parian, swallowed by the hollow trunks of twin oaks, marked entry to his grounds. The trees had grown side by side, two rare giants in the glorious countryside of olives and vineyards. Flanked by a plentiful river and boasting a spectacular view, it was the perfect place for a home. Oviello had been quite happy to stumble upon the ancient nymphaeum, whose grottos were fed by a bubbling mineral spring.

While they were lustful, wild creatures, Bel's brood were not altogether lacking in ingenuity or skills. Using clay from the nearby river banks Oviello crafted wondrous urns and amphorae, decorating them with lively paintings to pass the time. When the time of harvest came, everyone clamored for his wares, trading meats, cheeses and other staples for his pottery. It was a peaceful existence but the Satyroi were few. Without offspring, their kind would fade away and eventually die.

Children. The thought made his head ache. He didn't want to think about the little ones, but as a Keeper it was his responsibility to see that his brothers mated. The laughter of children had been absent for too many years. His father had sired the five of them and was at the sunset of his long life–wallowing in despair. None of his sons had found women. Only his sister, Daniella, had mated and long since left the sacred grove. She had left their ways behind, choosing to remain in the body of a human female, and as such had met an early death. With the decision to leave Bel's lands Daniella had also forsaken her long life. It had been a shame, but not so uncommon for his kind. Eventually even all the wine in the world could not ease the pain of loneliness.

Gently, Oviello set the girl down at the edge of the nymphaeum's marble pool, easing himself slowly into the cool water. Dipping beneath the water, he dunked his head backwards in a playful motion. It was all that was required to banish his troubled thoughts. Droplets trickled down his torso as he approached the limp girl, wondering whether to unshackle her from the dream.

The thin black cloth that wrapped around Gia's breasts was wet with perspiration. Oviello's eyes were drawn to her pale skin, the way it swelled deliciously beneath the garment. Oviello licked his canines with his tongue, anticipating the feel of her stiff, aching nipples in his mouth. He would let her sleep a while longer, he decided, drawing closer to slip the thin strap of the chemise down one shoulder.

Oviello weaved Gia's arms free of the straps, careful to be gentle. Tenderly, he pulled the top of the lacy camisole down, watching it cling to his captive's nipples before submitting to his wish. Oviello's body raged at the sight, blood quickening in his veins. The female's breasts were more beautiful than he could have imagined. Slightly puffy aureole rose to hardened nipples the color of dusky rose. Her breasts were pert and firm, succulent beneath the sheen film of sweat that glistened in the sun. By Bel, the scent of her desire wrapped around his mind with intoxicating bliss! For a moment his mind spun and he closed his eyes, searching for the patience to not devour her like the animal that he was.

Drinking in the sight of her perfect breasts and the swell of her ribs, Oviello caressed upwards to the line of her jaw. Elegant collarbones curved to the base of a slender neck. Tracing upwards he followed the slight cleft of her chin to pouty, parted lips that seemed soft and inviting. He imagined what it would be like to have those lips wrapped around his stiff cock, her dainty tongue seeking his. The girl's nose was smallish and pretty, curving elegantly towards beautiful, strong eyebrows the same color as her hair–her hair, by the gods, so lovely. It spilled over the marble edge and into the pool, radiant and glowing in the light like a honey halo. Oviello stroked a loose strand from her forehead, recalling the deep green of the woman's eyes, sparkling with wonder, as he had watched from a distance.

Pausing at the button of her shorts and the scrunched cami Oviello wondered how best to undress the slumbering girl without interrupting her dreams. Wickedly he smiled, easing himself out of the water. Oviello returned with a sharp knife which made quick work of her clothing. Removing her sandals, he gazed down at her naked glory. Gia's stomach dipped low and flared outwards to full hips. Her thighs were smooth, curved, supple. She was plump in all the right places, curvy and delicious. Between her outstretched thighs was a neatly trimmed triangle of brown hair, sticky and moist–ready to welcome his body. Surely he had snared a goddess, Oviello thought, setting the knife down.

Kneeling upon the edge of the pool, Oviello pushed her thighs apart, letting one of her legs dip into the cool water. Gia stirred but did not awaken. His body was like a bonfire and his heavy cock ached with desperation but he would not squander such a prize. No, he would savor her.

Placing his warm hands upon her upper thighs, Oviello used his thumbs to pry her nether lips open.

Slick softness parted to reveal the pink, succulent flesh of her entrance and the hard nub of her clit. Curiously, Oviello spread her open more fully, stretching her flesh wide. Could she accommodate him and his brothers? She was so tiny beneath him. At nearly seven feet he had the girth and length to match. Even the nymphs flung epithets to the gods when he mounted them.

Bending low he nuzzled his nose into her steamy entrance and inhaled her sweet scent. A wave of pleasure rolled through him, tightening his stomach. His cock jerked upwards, jutting proudly from his furry haunches. He nearly spilled his seed right then and there were it not for a judicious fist that clamped down around the base of his shaft. "Oh gods," Oviello whispered before nuzzling his nose into her vulnerable flesh. He slipped his long tongue into her slickness, curling it to draw out the nectar that dripped from her like honey. He guzzled her juices greedily, the tight grip on his cock growing ever more useless. Roughly he licked her, darting his tongue in and out with vicious need.

Under him, the slumbering girl shifted, pushing her hips upwards, thighs spread wide with unconscious need. Soft groans of pleasured bliss escaped her parted lips as Oviello guided Gia's dreams, allowing her to experience him between her legs in the guise of a human male. Small shudders coursed through her body as Gia clenched around his probing tongue. Writhing on the marble stone, still in the clutches of sleep, Gia climaxed, spilling her fragrant heat over his tongue.

Watching her writhe, tasting her ecstasy upon his lips, Oviello fisted his cock, knowing full well he would not last a single stroke inside her. The orgasm gripped him, shaking his body to the core. Pearly seed jetted out of him, spilling over his knuckles and her splayed thighs. Muscles rippling, breath ragged, Oviello milked his already-stiffening cock as he observed his captive with awe, pleased with his conquest.

Playfully, he caressed her nipples, massaging her globes with his large, rough hands. She felt so delicious, so soft and willing. Oviello was still incredibly aroused but the edge was off, allowing him to think more clearly. The female, he reminded himself, was his guest, not a prisoner. He would lavish upon her every indulgence, starting with a relaxing bath.

Gia groaned in dreamy bliss as the handsome, olive-skinned stranger eased himself from between her legs. He was tall, athletic, heavily muscled and divine! His amber eyes were a contrast to the darkness of his hair and his lips curved sensually into a wicked smile. She liked the way he looked at her. Under his hot gaze she felt radiant, desired–wanted. No man had ever looked at her this way–certainly none so gorgeous. Gia wanted him desperately–needed him to shove that gloriously huge cock inside her again. Over and over again, she thought, closing her eyes as he kissed invitingly along her thighs, inching closer to her center of pleasure.

The delightful dream slowly faded, leaving Gia giggling upon a marble dais, with naught but a simple pillow to support her head. Slowly, she opened her eyes to meet her mysterious lover's laughing gaze. Oviello kissed gently up along her naked thigh, his features obscured in the semi-darkness of the hidden grotto. Disconcerted, uncertain if she was still dreaming, Gia blinked, unwilling to tear her gaze from his. Her body felt languid and soft, as if she'd been floating in a bed of rose petals. All around her the sound of falling water mingled with the scent of olive and pine. Gone was the grove, the sunlight and... Hadrian's Villa!

Startled, Gia sat up, eyes wide, to find she was naked, slippery and utterly turned on. Her mind scrambled as she tried to make sense of the surroundings. Past the shadows she glimpsed stairs leading down to the opening of a cave, shielded from sunlight by a curtain of rushing water. Ferns trembled beneath the deluge and a cool breeze caressed her skin.

The deliciously attractive man slowly lifted his palms in a gesture of non-aggression. Without making any sudden moves Gia turned her attention to the stranger. Had she been raped? Her body felt radiant and pleasured, the slickness between her legs a testament to—. "You are still dreaming," she told herself, a half whisper in the half light. Only in a dream could she hope to land in such a gorgeous place with such a gorgeous guy.

Sparkling reflections from the water revealed a golden, mosaic-encrusted dome above her head. Lapis, jade, obsidian and gold were woven into weathered friezes—pastoral scenes resembling the ones she had seen in the museums of Rome. The scenes depicted slaves bearing platters of fruit and urns of wine, satyrs playing flutes, men and women reclining in benches amidst an ornate wood. Bacchanalia, she believed Valentino had called the feast that venerated the god of wine.

Gia was in the center of a circular room upon a carved, raised marble dais. All around her were trays of fruit and colorfully painted urns and she could smell the heady scent of wine mingling with oil. The quiet stranger from her dreams knelt at the foot of her stone bed, his arms still raised—amber eyes scanning hers.

Speechless, Gia realized that she was slick from head to toe and covered in oil. She traced the stone with her fingers finding it slippery and warm from her body heat. She covered her breasts with her arms and closed her legs, blushing hotly under the man's intense gaze. Aroused, with blood beating at her temples, Gia's words fled.

Slowly Oviello lowered his hands, gauging her reaction. The girl did not seem overly startled and for that he was glad. He brought a palm to his chest and tapped, his voice echoing in the hollowness. *"Salve, mihi nomen est Oviello."*

Gia knew he wasn't speaking English or Italian but somehow understood. "Oviello," she said swallowing hard, the sound of his voice rolling through her like an earthquake, "my name is Giovanna. How did I get here?"

Oviello wondered whether he should tell her the truth. There would be no point in keeping the girl against her will. He continued to talk in the strange language but somehow the words were once again clear. "You wandered into my lands and fell asleep beneath the punishing sun. I brought you to my home wishing the pleasure of your company."

The words were formal and archaic, the phrasing lacking modern mannerism, but Gia grasped their meaning regardless. Gia's heart stammered in her chest as she wondered how she had wound up naked and oiled like a Sunday roast in a cave with some wild-looking hunk of a man who was, very, very happy to see her. Her cheeks burned hotly as she spied the flared, moist tip of his erect phallus pressed between the edge of the bed and his belly button. Oviello was huge, more animal than man.

The man had sequestered her, stripped her naked and... had had his way with her? Gia clenched her thighs more tightly as images from the desirous dream flooded her mind, igniting her lust. The air between them sizzled with unseen energy. Danger seemed to emanate from the man's imposing build and yet Gia was mesmerized.

Gia thought of the hotel room in Tivoli and her backpack and passport and of all the practical things in her life like her family, the job, the apartment and a million other things but as Oviello's hands made contact with her feet, gently massaging the oil into her skin, the worries faded. She could scream and run or choose to indulge the moment. The man who called himself Oviello was something out of a dream. A straight nose, regal and noble, led down to sensually full lips and a proud chin, chiseled like the rest of him. His dark hair, braided in places with bits of leather and leaves, was wild and unkempt, yet soft as it brushed over her legs. Each kiss upon her skin sent a delightful tremor along her middle. His touch was heavenly.

Gia had a million questions but her body ached only for one answer—how he'd feel fully sheathed inside her. Relaxing back into his kisses she closed her eyes. If Oviello was a dream, she hoped never to awaken. If he wasn't, she hoped he would stick around at least until breakfast and not run out on her in the middle of the night.

Pleased by her surrender, Oviello resumed his worship, hoping that Gia might, after being pleasured, not care that he was not entirely human. He had chosen the spot wisely. The grotto was lit only by the flickering reflections and much too dark for her to see his true nature. He was Satyroi, half beast, half man—the plaything of the gods—but kneeling as he was beneath the tall dais, he allowed Gia to see only enough to whet her appetite.

Lightly, his loving fingers coaxed the tension from her limbs. He worked slowly, soothing the soles of her feet and her smooth calves, occasionally venturing higher until his hands crossed the invisible line of her knees. Oviello observed her, measuring her reactions, proceeding gently, careful not to startle her. He was amazed by the girl's willingness to trust him but was prepared fully for retaliation.

Gia lay still, mind racing as she allowed the intimidating stranger to massage her legs. Should she run? Hide? Call for help? The rational woman inside her chastised herself for her willingness to take the risk while the romantic yearned for his hands to climb ever higher. Her body pleaded for his touch even as her mind rebelled. Eyes still closed, Gia did her best to relax but her ragged breaths caught at the back of her throat. As the hands wandered over her thighs she reached out and grasped them. If she was going to surrender she wanted to do so on her terms–not as some unwilling victim but as a joyful partner. It had been too long since she had been loved, never mind worshipped, and this man seemed to have every intention of worshipping her.

Oviello stopped, a ripple of fire coursing through his veins as Gia's hands glided over his. A willing captive of the girl's next move, Oviello held his breath–hoping. As Gia's long lashes fluttered open to reveal the brilliant green of her eyes, time stood still. Green and amber met as they locked gazes, the air sizzling between them.

"You will not hurt me?" she whispered, eyes questioning–pleading.

Oviello was transfixed, realizing there was hope in the inquiry. His thumbs gently caressed her knuckles. "I wish only to please you, if you allow it."

Gia heard the words but it was the yearning in his voice that convinced her. Whoever the stranger before her was, he was lonely like her–desperate like her. Lust mingled with fear as she drew up his hands to kiss his knuckles. Gia's voice nearly cracked, sounding tiny and pathetic, but there was a quiet strength behind the words. "I know nothing about you, nor where I find myself, but," she dragged his hands along the top of her thighs, drawing him closer, "I want you."

The admission was lightning. Oviello's world spun. In an instant he was upon her, his body cleaving to hers. Braced on his elbows, he sank into her embrace, his dark hair falling over them as his mouth found hers. The kiss was wild and immediate. Gia's hands reached under his shoulders to caress his back, pulling him closer, seeking more and more of him as his tongue sought hers. Never had she felt so utterly lost in a man– so deliriously wanton. Insisting hips pushed forward until his rock-hard shaft was pressed hotly against her oil-slick belly. "Yes," she crooned into his mouth as she devoured his sweet kiss, her tongue dancing with his.

Gia's small hands caressed urgently along the length of his body, finally settling on his ass. When that wasn't enough, she wrapped her thighs around his hips in an effort to pull their bodies closer. Oblivious to her effect on him, Gia followed her instincts, bucking her hips upwards as she sought her own pleasure. A blissful wave of ecstasy rippled through her slick body as Oviello licked along her lips, savoring her taste. Caught in the throes of lust, Gia failed to notice the fur along Oviello's muscled haunches, or the horns that lurked beneath the braided hair.

Oviello's self-control was nearly obliterated by the girl's moans. He sucked on her tongue and nibbled on her lips, unwilling to end the kiss. Her mouth was as succulent as the rest of her. She was bucking wildly beneath him, seeking release, her slick buttocks sliding upon the marble as she sought more and more of him. He grinned above her, parting with her lips to sink his face down into the crook of her neck. Sharp teeth grazed the flesh before his tongue soothed it. Oviello licked her neck and nibbled on her ear, raising his hips just slightly so that she would have to work her body higher to seek his length.

Their bodies collided time and time again—hot flesh against flesh. Manacled, they groped and kissed, hips daring hips until at last one of them gave in. Gia gripped his hair and pleaded, whispering hotly against his ear, "Please..."

Oviello smiled in the darkness, nodding. She would get what she wanted and more but not before he had his fill. He would be glad to remind her, when he tasted her tears of pleasure, that she had, indeed, begged.

The satyr detached himself from her limbs and kneeled between her legs, using his thighs to spread the girl wide open. Gone was the fear and trepidation. Oviello saw only desire when he looked upon Gia's flushed body and half-closed eyes. He intended to finish what he had started. Picking up a jar of oil, he tipped it over until a golden thread of it met her skin.

Gasping and out of air, breasts heaving, Gia pouted, wondering what he was up to. Oviello massaged the oil into her body, quieting her protests with an index finger before returning to his task. Inching forward, he positioned himself far enough for only the tip of his cock to graze her clit. The slick heat of her cunt was sweet torture but Oviello's determination to drive her wild offered him a modicum of self-control. He began at her neck, using his powerful hands to ply the tenseness from her tense muscles, gliding his hands down over her beautifully sculpted shoulders. He worked the warm oil over the taut muscles of her arms, each of his movements prodding her sensitive bud. With a will of their own, Gia's hips slid downwards so that little by little, as he worked her body, she nudged his thickness slowly inside her.

The satyr flashed Gia a smirk, purposely avoiding the girl's nipples as his hands circled the globes of her breasts. Gia didn't care that she was displayed before him, her body at his whim. Even the tip of his cock felt impossibly large inside her but with every stroke of his hands she craved more.

Oviello allowed her to take him slowly, using the massage as a ruse to introduce her to his girth. Plunging into her would have only caused pain and he wanted her willingness and desire. Oviello's expert hands traversed her body, feasting on her flesh. Gia was warm and soft, firm in the right places, melting under his touch. He felt surrounded by her, felt the urge to plunder her spread, curvy body, tantalizingly supine. Oviello could feel her stretching and clutching until at last her tight channel gave way. Gia sank a little further towards him, hot and wet, at the brink of an orgasm. Oviello was so aroused he could barely breathe. Steadying his hips was a monumental task. Gia had taken more than half his length when she groaned, nails digging into his arms.

Instantly, Oviello's hands were upon her thighs, thumbs traveling up and down the edges of her labia. He felt every tiny spasm along his shaft, knew full well how explosive the orgasm building inside her would be. Gia gasped, struggling to remain still. Her mysterious lover was keen on torturing her. It was by far the most attention she had ever received from a man and Gia was wondering if that was a good thing or not. Her body was at the brink of an earthquake, a tidal wave, wound tight by the sensual massage and made worse by Oviello's avoidance of sensitive areas.

Gia had taken his cock slowly and even as such felt herself stretched wide open. Oviello was stunningly beautiful and possessed the patience of a saint. She wanted him to take her over the edge but was afraid of breaking the spell. Was he a dream? She was slick and moist all over, slipping and sliding along the marble bed as he continued to work her. In Oviello's eyes she saw something more than desire and it both scared and thrilled her.

There was a wild, woodsy scent about him—something untamed and wicked. When he smiled Gia spied long canines. It didn't occur to her that he wasn't a man at all until her hands found his thighs. Where there should have been flesh there was soft fur. It's a dream, Gia thought, so close to an orgasm she could have cared less if he was the devil himself. Panting, Gia gripped Oviello's furry thighs, edging closer to the base of his shaft.

Oviello slid deep, watching the girl beneath him shudder needfully. When Gia's tight body clenched around him, it nearly took his breath away. Oviello had teased her beyond the point where most females would have tried to scratch his eyes out. Such fortitude deserved just reward. With a single thrust, he buried himself inside her as his hands kneaded her breasts. Oviello pulled the taut flesh until he held the tips of her nipples captive between thumb and index finger. Again he rocked his hips, forcing her open to allow him full passage.

Under him, Gia groaned as her lover toyed with her perky nipples, the pain of the invading phallus sharp as Oviello thrust deep into her. The satyr tortured her aching breasts, pulling and teasing the stiff peaks, rolling the nubs in his fingers so roughly it made her wince. It was just enough pressure to distract her from the ache as he settled fully inside her.

The pain mingled with the pleasure so seamlessly Gia nearly screamed. Tears welled up in her eyes and he held her still, allowing her body time to adjust. "By the gods," he growled, fighting the urge to ravage her, "Giovanna..."

Her name sounded foreign and beautiful in his strange language. It was as if through its utterance Oviello had somehow changed the very nature of who she was. She was no longer Gia the textile buyer but some other woman—a free spirit who was no longer afraid of living.

As Oviello rubbed her slippery clit, Gia's hands flew to her breasts, pulling and massaging herself into oblivion. The orgasm rose from the deepest, most dormant parts of Gia's being. It heralded the release of a long-shackled soul as much as of a long-ignored body. Gia felt beautiful and radiant, connected to the river of life. Her body convulsed and her hips bucked arrhythmically under Oviello's ministrations. Eyes closed and lips half parted, Gia gasped and groaned, impaled on the massive cock as waves of searing heat crested and fell against her senses. She was sent careening to some distant, wonderful place she had never known, feeling warm, wanted, deliciously sore and needing more.

Gripping both sides of the stone bed, all Oviello had to do to coax another scream of desire was to insinuate his weight between her outstretched legs. Gia felt wonderful, so small and tight he could barely fit inside her. Beads of sweat broke upon his lower back as he controlled his movements so as not to hurt her. Gently, Oviello pumped his hips, self-control eroding with every thrust.

Like a cat in heat, Gia set her nails into Oviello's sides. She pulled at him with lustful moans as another orgasm wracked her frame. "More!" Gia begged, tears streaming from her eyes as her cunt milked his throbbing body.

Oviello rode the girl's climax steadily, claiming her hungry mouth, swallowing the gasps and moans until he felt her tightness ease. Feeling that she was ready, Oviello plunged into her with all of his passion, fists coiling in her honey tresses. Their bodies crashed at a frenzied pace as desire finally conquered caution. Throwing cares to the wind the lovers fucked, rutting like animals, their moans fueling their lust. Oviello gripped Gia's waist and to Gia's surprise she found his horns and held on. Her body had never been so well used, so fully pleasured.

Every tear of pain and pleasure was kissed away as the satyr slammed his hips into the girl cradled in his powerful embrace. If truly the Elysian Fields existed, Oviello had found them. Strength surged through his body as he pulled Gia upwards to straddle his hips. He knelt with her, gripping her beautiful ass and spreading her wide, watching her glorious breasts jiggle as he had his way.

As the impending, blinding rush of orgasm tightened his balls, Oviello buried his face in Gia's neck, inhaling her sweet, exotic scent. He pumped blindly, seeking release, his senses utterly consumed, trembling with need. Gia's body felt as it would be split in half by the monstrously large prick that invaded her. She had lost count of the orgasms Oviello had given her and wanted nothing more than to feel his hot seed surge into her womb. The man or beast who clung to her had pleasured her beyond reproach and she desired to do the same.

Oviello panted as his whole body shook. With one final, decisive thrust, he brought the girl down roughly, burying himself to the hilt. Jets of his cum flooded her tightness, filling her with delicious warmth. He growled, honeyed eyes glowing in the gloom as he held onto his prize, muscles locking as the orgasm sapped his strength.

Gia wrapped her arms around Oviello's shoulders and relaxed, loving the feel of him inside her. She felt spent and weak, satisfied in spite of the splitting soreness between her legs. It was a strange, wonderful feeling to feel the sticky warmth between them. Their combined juices dripped from between her legs and she smiled, kissing her lover shyly along the scruff of his cheek. Oviello held her protectively close. There was a tenderness to the embrace that differed from the way any of her past lovers had treated her. Gia didn't care what Oviello was, only that he had loved her–truly loved her.

They clung to each other for a long time, afraid to let go, their breathing the only sound rivaling the rushing water. Giovanna was not the only one who thought she was dreaming. Oviello thought it also, wondering if the woman in his arms would vanish if he released her. He had been afraid he'd hurt her but Gia's loving kisses placated his fears. "Are you a dream?" he asked, his voice a seductive purr against her ear.

Gia smiled, resting her head on his shoulder, idle fingers tracing slow circles upon his skin. "Are you?"

Oviello cursed his desire as he stood with Gia in his arms. Still inside her, he sat at the edge of the bed and reclined gently back. The feel of her straddled above him was delightful. Gia's question would have been easy to answer were it not for the fact that he was, in many ways, part of a world unseen. "I am what you wish me to be," he replied, his hands gliding up along her thighs.

Gia sighed, her body languid. "Are you Italian? Because if you are you should pinch me now and maybe I will wake up."

A low chuckle rolled through Oviello's chest. He squeezed her closer, instantly reminding her of his growing desire. "My grove does border Hadrian's Villa so by that definition I suppose I am Italian."

Gia's eyelids felt heavy along with her body. She might as well have been run over by a truck. She couldn't believe her newfound lover wanted more and so soon. Maybe Italian guys weren't such a good idea. Still, in the past she had made love for hours and never felt so utterly exhausted. Gia was positively drained. "Never mind about that pinch," she mumbled, snuggling against him, "I don't know that I want to know what you really are."

"Sleep," Oviello whispered, pulling her up against his chest as he slid out of her. He had grown to his full length in a matter of minutes and was ready yet again. Oviello brushed his hair back and stared at the ceiling, the feel of the woman intoxicating. His captive was handling his reality much better than he had hoped but with every passing day, she would question more. He had no right to keep her and yet he had.

The satyr stroked the tired girl softly and sang an ancient tune, lulling Gia's body into a state of blissful oblivion. His voice carried her to a distant place of dreams where together, they frolicked amidst flowering fields. Happily he weaved the sunlight and the trees, the stream, the butterflies. Oviello gave himself powerful legs and feet and became the image of her deepest fantasy. He was Italian and bore the trappings of her contemporary life, faded blue jeans and an open white shirt, yet he smelled familiar, of woods and wilds. Gia's hair was loose in the breeze and she finally caught up to him, laughing. How she loved him! It was a dream worthy of a lifetime.

Oviello closed his eyes. "Dreams," he whispered regretfully in the darkness, "just dreams, Giovanna."

Even through closed lids Oviello sensed the shadow that crossed the gushing water. It was Navid, his youngest brother, who bore the scent of the river upon his skin. Oviello did not turn nor did he cease stroking the limp girl upon his chest. "You arrive too soon, Navid," Oviello said somberly.

The hulking satyr took a step forward, climbing the threshold. "Too soon? Brother, honored Keeper, I am last in all things and you would deny me this?"

Oviello sighed. "She is mortal and fragile, we have taken too much already."

"Yes, you have all taken, all three of you, and yet here I stand, unsatisfied!"

The Keeper grit his teeth at his brother's impertinence. Sharing the female amongst his brothers had been a poor choice but so had been luring the girl from her intended path. Oviello had made certain Gia had been pleasured but he could not defy the laws of his people. Sharing her had ensured he'd be able to enjoy her freely without fear of his brothers' enmity. Selfishly, Oviello had concealed the girl's existence for many days before alerting the others. With offers to Bel, Oviello prayed that his seed grew in Gia's belly but only time would tell. "Come," he said to the young satyr, parting Gia's thighs, "have your turn."

In two graceful bounds Navid closed the distance, his body eager. He knelt upon the bench between his brother's and Gia's spread legs and rubbed her dripping slit with two of his fingers, his mouth watering. "I've never had a mortal woman," he admitted, somewhat uncertainly, "are they like the nymphs?"

Oviello watched him. "No, they are not. She is much smaller and you must be gentle."

"She cannot pleasure me," Navid said, dismayed at how soundly Gia slept. "You keep her in the waking hours for yourself. Does she even know what we are?"

The young satyr spread her ass cheeks, gazing down at her. Slowly he slid a finger into her well-oiled rear and smiled. "I see there are still ways I can leave my mark."

Oviello shook his head. His younger brother was much too eager to prove himself. "I am sorry to disappoint you, dear brother, Naias left no part of her undiscovered."

"Naias was here? What of Ariano? Am I always the last in your thoughts?"

Oviello smiled, stroking Gia's arms. "Do not be cross with me, you know the rules, Navid, stop sulking and make her yours."

Navid pushed another finger into her tight hole, enjoying her tightness as he rubbed the tip of his cock against her slick folds. With a delirious moan he pushed inside the sleeping girl, continuing to tease her ass. "Weave this into her dreams, brother, so that at least she might know me. Weave your spells!"

Sunlight streamed across the fields as Gia lay on Oviello's lap. She giggled softly as her lover teased her, struggling in vain to lower her skirt. Oviello's shoulder-length hair blew haphazardly in the wind as he squinted, looking into the distance. Gia followed his gaze, finally succeeding in dissuading wandering fingers.

"My brother comes to join us," Oviello said, smiling.

"I didn't know you had a brother," she said, sitting up properly.

"I have three brothers and a sister, though she passed away."

Gia lowered her eyes, realizing she barely knew anything about him. "I'm sorry."

Oviello traced the line of her jaw and smiled, his eyes sincere. "Don't be, it was a long time ago."

Gia doted on Oviello's sun-kissed beauty, imagining how thrilled her mother would be that she had found a gorgeous guy in Italy. New York seemed like a fading memory—a faraway place. Secretly, she felt a pang of joy. "I like it here," she said, a wicked look crossing her eyes.

"I'm glad. Would you ever consider staying?"

"I think so," she said without thinking.

Oviello claimed her lips in a brief kiss. "You will forget about me, no doubt. I am just your vacation romance."

Gia wrinkled her nose, not having thought about the future. "According to experts, vacation crushes are the worst to get over," she chided. "What's to say you won't forget about me?"

"Never," he said, his amber eyes meeting hers.

The feeling in his words shook her. Oviello was the most intense human being she had ever met. He could make her melt with a word, a look, a caress. Smiling, she sized him up. "Your English is much better than my Italian. Think you can fit in my suitcase?"

Oviello chuckled, slapping her ass playfully. "We can teach you Italian in no time! Come, let me introduce you to my brother." With lightning quickness, he leaped to his feet and trotted down the hill.

Gia watched the two men clasp hands in the distance. They were a sight! Tall and thin, the younger man had the face of an angel and a mouth so seductive it nearly took her breath away. His honey-colored, sun-bathed hair danced in the wind as he strode confidently in her direction. He was possibly the second most attractive man she had ever seen and the image of them together was like something out of *GQ Magazine*. Gia nearly giggled at the thought of her job. If they could see her now, she thought, basking in the Italian countryside, drinking wine with two delicious-looking Italian guys. Blushing, she grinned, grateful for the wine that warmed her belly as the dashing pair neared.

Grinning widely Oviello dove next to her, nipping playfully at her neck. "Meet my brother, Gia," he said with an outstretched hand in the younger man's direction.

As if on cue, the younger man bowed with exaggerated flair. "Ciao, Bella!" he said, half-jesting, allowing his lips to linger on the back of Gia's slender hand.

The touch made her heart race. "Hi, I'm Gia, *un piacere*," she stammered, quickly snatching her hand from his grasp.

"Navid," he said with a wink, plopping himself down beside them, a devious glint in his eyes.

Oviello grinned, enjoying her shyness. "Careful with my brother, he's quite the ladies' man."

"Oh really?" she mused, her body growing inexplicably hot under their combined stares.

"My brother has told me so much about you, frankly I am curious," said Navid, his smiling eyes turning to Oviello.

Still blushing, Gia straightened, nearly jumping when Navid's hand grazed hers. Curious, indeed, she thought, casting a wry glance at Oviello whose crooked half-smile was fraught with amusement. "And what has he told you?"

Navid inched closer, allowing his fingers to overtly caress her forearm. "Everything."

Sitting opposite his brother, Oviello smiled, gently brushing Gia's hair aside. He leaned in and whispered sweetly in her ear, his voice deep and husky, "Do you like my brother Giovanna?"

Nervously, Gia shifted, again withdrawing from Navid's touch. The tease in her lover's voice was incredibly sexy. How did she get herself into this situation? Was she on the verge of a threesome with two hot Italian men? Brothers? Did she understand that correctly? Were they both coming on to her? Gia's heart leaped to her throat and she felt suddenly naked beneath their scorching gazes. Sweat burst from every pore and the sun suddenly seemed unbearable. "Is it hot out here or is it just me?" she asked, feeling instantly ridiculous.

Deep, heartfelt laughter bellowed from both men, making her embarrassment worse. Gia wanted to run and hide but instead she joined them, their combined laughter resounding in the glorious meadow. Slowly, they recovered, the giggles dying down to wicked smirks. Gia eased into Oviello's embrace, enjoying the safety of his arms.

Across from them, Navid reclined on an elbow, his eyes growing serious as he watched them. As quickly as the laughter had passed, silence grew between them. Navid's eyes devoured her, traveling along the length of her curves. It was a sweet caress that ignited with its intensity. Under the seductive gaze, Gia felt wonderful, as if every inch of her were alive.

Behind her, Oviello smiled, nudging his chin in the direction of the wine. Navid rolled over and grabbed the bottle, opening it with practiced flair. He poured the liquid evenly into three glasses, a smile dancing on his lips. "Do the honors, dear brother," he said, handing them both a glass.

Oviello shifted, running the edge of the glass suggestively against Gia's arm. "To the bane of love!" he said, kissing Gia's shoulder.

Gia clinked their glasses, sipping deeply, the warmth of the wine blossoming in her belly. "Don't believe in love, do you?" she asked shyly, feeling a tingle travel down her spine.

Unexpectedly, Oviello's free hand trailed along her thigh until it found the all-too-familiar spot under her skirt. Seeking fingers pushed against the moist cotton of her panties. Gia tried to dissuade the caress but before she could, Navid was upon her, his body pressing insistently against her side. When she tried to move away she felt a strong arm around her upper arm. "Stay," came Navid's sultry voice as his grip tightened.

Gia's heart tripped. Never in a million years had it crossed her mind that she would be the type of woman to allow such a thing, but in a few days she would be on a plane and the sunny skies of Italy would be long gone. Swallowing hard, she mustered courage, taking a long sip of the heady wine before setting the glass down.

It was the only answer Gia could give as nerves claimed her tongue. It was answer enough. Navid inched closer, boldly dragging her hand along his leg. Her fingers curled in protest but eased over the bulge in his pants. Gia sucked in her breath, the forwardness catching her off guard. Slowly, her palm caressed the taut fabric, her entire body burning in the summer heat. There was no disguising the sudden arousal that welled up inside her, making her ache with need. It was insanity and she didn't care.

Oviello smiled, watching the two, his fingers pressing into the folds of her pussy through the thin cotton panties. He circled her clit with deliberate patience, applying pressure as he buried his face between her ample breasts. With his teeth he dragged the strapless dress down, popping a breast free.

Gia gasped, her natural reaction to cover herself but again her hand was pulled back. Navid moaned against her neck, his hand over hers as he urged her to feel the extent of his need. *"Bella,"* he whispered, nuzzling against her ear, "my brother tells me you are leaving in a few days. Is this true?"

The cool air felt wonderful against her skin as the other side of the dress was pulled down. Oviello rubbed her slickness as he closed his mouth around a nipple, biting the tip before sucking it into his mouth. Gia moaned, the sudden heat clouding her thoughts. "Yesss," she stammered, her hand squeezing Navid's length through the fabric "I... I have a job in New York that I need to get back to."

Oviello's tongue lathed the hard nipple, his fingers skirting the fabric to stroke her exquisite heat. In one push he slid two fingers inside her, teasing her as his brother pulled her gently back.

Navid bent over the panting girl until his mouth nearly touched hers, his breath hot as he spoke. "Have you ever been loved by two lovers, Gia?"

Self-conscious, yet half-mad with desire, Gia shook her head. The no that was ripped from her throat was a word of desperation, a plea for them to stop and simultaneously continue.

"We will worship you well past the point where you forget about New York," purred Oviello, sinking his fingers inside her to the knuckles.

Above her the younger man smiled before crushing his mouth to hers, his eager tongue seeking satisfaction. Gia accepted the kiss without reservation, her arms wrapping around the man's neck in a passionate embrace. A wicked, insatiable longing swelled inside her as she heard the clinking sound of his belt being unbuckled. Navid devoured her lips, licking and sucking her tongue, his hand finding the globe of her breast.

The decadence of being locked between them thrilled her. Gia felt completely outside of herself, lost in a sea of desire as her lovers grew bolder. Oviello pushed the skirt upwards until it bunched at her waist. Gripping the dress with one fist, he wedged his shoulders between her thighs until she was splayed. Hungrily he pushed forward, dragging her soaked panties to the side before jamming his tongue into her sticky heat. He flicked her clit with a flurry of quick licks until her hips rose with a will of their own. Only then did he reward her juicy slit with two probing fingers. He fucked her slow but deep as his devilish brother pinched her nipples, rolling them between his fingers.

Navid sucked on the girl's tongue, savoring the feel of her in his hands. Her breasts were plump and full, like ripe fruits. She was a delight to the senses in the summer heat and every moan threatened his self-control. The sight of her spread legs and the glistening moisture that built beneath his brother's tongue coaxed a tortured groan from the depths of his chest. "Gia," he growled, releasing his cock from the confines of his pants, "your mouth. Please..."

Gia's eyes met Navid's for a split second before they settled on his shaft. He was thick, nearly as large as his brother. His hair was trimmed neatly, tapering to a delectable treasure trail that ran upwards along washboard abs. Lean and sculpted, graced with caramel skin, Navid was like something out of a wicked daydream. She was as drawn to him as she was to the man that knelt between her legs. Brothers, she thought, the wrongness filling her with decadent wantonness as she drew closer.

Navid's chest rose and fell with anticipation as he gazed into her eyes. Desire could not have been more plainly written on her parted lips. Slowly he peeled his shirt off, pleased when her eyes darted to his muscled body. Teasingly he ran his hands along the curve of her face, grazing her lips with his thumb. *"Ti voglio,"* he whispered, stroking his cock until a bead of moisture glistened at its tip.

Gia gasped when Oviello turned her around and brought her up, raising her to all fours. Hastily, her lover undid his pants and discarded his shirt, positioning himself behind her. The heat between her legs rivaled the afternoon sun as she parted her thighs, anxious to be filled. Powerful hands gripped the globes of her ass before thumbs sank into her dripping cunt. Oviello edged her slippery flesh, coaxing her open. Gia moaned, surrendering to her hunger, her tongue reaching out to taste the offered cock.

A lustful shiver coursed up Navid's spine as Gia's inviting tongue made contact, tasting and licking along the underside of his cock. He jerked against her lips—thick and aching with lust. Behind her, Oviello watched, enthralled with the feel of her tightness. Up and down he rubbed the swollen mound, using his cock as an instrument of exquisite torture.

Gia's hips followed Oviello's motions as dewy lips closed around Navid's length. With a near growl Oviello pushed himself inside her, thrusting her forward until she was impaled on both ends, his brother's cock buried deep in her mouth.

Navid wrapped his fists in the girl's hair, his lust soaring. Gently he rocked his hips, easing himself into her hungry mouth. The desire between them sizzled in the noon-day sun. Eyes locked together, the two brothers took advantage of Gia's willingness to please.

Two lovers at once was a feat of concentration. For a few minutes Gia attempted to keep a rhythm, the palms of her hands serving to assuage Navid's insistent hips, but her efforts soon fell to the wayside. With every push into her small body, Oviello unleashed his lustful fury, causing her to lose control. Through choked moans and trembling thighs Gia pleasured them, her mind devoid of all thought save for the thrilling spasms that coursed the length of her body. She was only dimly aware of bracing herself so as not to fall forward, the muscles in her arms flexing until they ached. Pleasure and pain mingled in an exquisite symphony.

Gia sucked and licked, ground her hips back until she was completely out of herself–a pure instrument of blissful pleasure. Hands caressed her moist chin, flowed through her hair, shoulders, hips, ass, thighs. She could not tell where one man began and the other ended. Beads of sweat formed between her bouncing breasts, the crook of her neck, between her thighs. The thickness that invaded her claimed her fully, the fingers that rubbed her clit wicked in their expertise.

Navid's thighs flexed as he arched back, releasing her but for a moment. His belly quivered and his body tensed. Gia gripped his hips blindly, unwilling to stop until the man screamed at the sky. A thunderous growl rumbled through his chest as Navid's body shook, trembling, sweat-slick hair clinging to his shoulders.

It was a strange feeling, wanting to please without reserve, without thought or judgment. Gia sucked violently, soft lips gripping Navid's spurting cock. She milked his copious, creamy release, swallowing as much as she could–wanting every drop.

Before her, the glorious man eased somewhat, the tension slowly draining from his body. Hunger and awe blazed in his gaze and for a moment Gia thought she might drown forever in that azure ocean. Heart beating wildly, cheeks and breasts flushed with heat, she was a woman transformed. It was liberating to languish in her lover's ecstasy, claiming his pleasure as if it were her own.

A delicious surge of heat coursed through her as she was pounded mercilessly from behind. She gripped Navid's hardness in her fist and stroked, sucking in her breath in frantic gulps. The fingers that teased between her legs were incessant, Oviello knew her too well.

Each of Gia's sweet, clenching spasms sent pulses of delightful pleasure along her flesh. She was so filled she thought she might be split in half–her arms no longer able to bear the weight of her body. She collapsed forward, shoulders to the blanket, Navid's cock still in hand, hips raised wantonly.

The sight of her raised rump, of his cock disappearing time and time again in her heated sheath, was unbearable. Oviello pinched Gia's clit, flicking rapidly, feeling her channel tighten ever more with her frantic heat. Words and thoughts escaped him, all consciousness fleeing until there was nothing but her liquid embrace. Oviello fucked her to his own oblivion, her moans and screams music to his ears.

Beneath Oviello, Gia writhed, her nails digging into Navid's thighs, as the orgasm erased all reason. Gia was powerless to stop the deluge of pleasure. The orgasm unfolded deep inside her and blossomed, filling her in ways she never thought possible. A cry caught at her throat to finally become a scream–a prayer to some unknown god as she struggled in vain to halt Oviello's torturous fingers. Even before the first wave of pleasure ended another crested. Thus Oviello held her, suspended in that peak of climax until tears welled up and spilled.

Driven wild with desire for the sighing, panting girl whose body swallowed his, Oviello pushed on, oblivious to pleading hands that begged his fingers to ease. Across from them, Navid stared enviously, his cock jutting proudly between his legs. He was ignored by the rutting couple until the word, "Brother," grated past clenched teeth.

Oviello's gaze fell on Navid as he pulled on the girl beneath him, causing her thighs to squeeze together. "She's mine!" Oviello snarled, pushing into her with a brutal thrust.

"Even in a dream you cannot give me the pleasure?"

"You test my patience, Navid!"

"Release her, you selfish prick, and let me take her."

Oviello maintained his tempo, his cock aching for release. "You will have her after I've had my fill. Do not forget your place."

It was in those throes, those confusing words between brothers and lovers, that Gia let go, her body throbbing with every unforgiving crash of his hips. The man behind her was possessed in a fury and she was his captive. Gia felt small beneath him, clinging to the blankets, her heart racing as her lungs sought frantically to catch up. Her thighs burned along with her arms and yet the soreness was a Godsend. Gia found peace wedged between her two lovers, the kind of peace that came after a grueling day of hard work. Was it her body or her mind that surrendered? Both? She could not be sure.

Hands gripped her waist and pulled. Over and over again Gia was claimed in that summer heat, in that idyllic countryside where her grandparents had surely met. Thoughts and memories collided and merged with Oviello's moans. Gia barely recalled she had a home and a job in a faraway place. Her fists closed around the fabric beneath her but it felt smooth like stone.

She heard words, arguments perhaps, but could not be certain. She was invaded, pleasured, teased, touched, kissed. Behind her Oviello bent over her, his arms rippling as he gasped for breath. Warmth engulfed her womb as her lover finally found release, clinging to her, breath hot against her neck. Oviello was heaven made flesh, and the words that he whispered in that moment, a reason for living.

They were ancient words, neither English or Italian, but she understood them, felt them in every fiber of her being. She wanted them to be true as she closed her eyes, spent and breathless.

"You are mine," Oviello whispered, kissing the sweat from her temple, the length of his body heavy as he lay over her, "mine."

Navid's body arched protectively over the girl as he sated his lust a third time. Gently, he eased himself over her, grinding his hips to the hilt, grateful that his brother had at last left him to enjoy his turn. The mortal woman was different from the nymphs, smaller and more fragile, but there was something else that called to his ancient heritage. Navid had felt her in his blood; had felt their merging in ways he never thought possible.

Carefully he withdrew, making sure to squeeze every last drop of his seed inside her. "Unlike my brother, dear goddess," he said huskily against her ear, "I am quite sure I want offspring."

Grinning, Navid reclined against the length of her body, his head propped on one elbow. He gazed down at her flushed body, pausing at the sight of her scrumptious dark-tipped breasts. Lazily he toyed with a nipple before massaging the creamy globe. "Soon they will be ripe with milk and we will all feast upon you." Navid released the breast and watched the supple flesh jiggle, wickedness dancing in his gaze. Leaning forward he nuzzled Gia's ear, his warm palm idly stroking her hips. "You will serve us well, bear us many children," he promised, sliding his fingers inside her sore body.

Oviello's deep resonant voice echoed in the darkness of the cavern. "Have you had enough?" he asked, his cloven steps echoing upon the marble.

"Enough? As if, brother! Look at her," Navid replied, his body already growing hard and ready.

Oviello's eyes lingered upon Navid's fingers as they sank in the sticky triangle of curls between Gia's thighs. Arms crossed, Oviello took a step forward. "Although it pains me, I am going to release her."

Navid shot up, sitting on the edge of the stone bed. "What?"

"You heard me, Navid. We cannot keep her, not like this."

"Like what?"

"I will not continue to weave the dreams."

"You must."

"No."

Navid threw up his hands, exasperated. "Do you not want her?"

Oviello sidestepped his brother. With an easy grace he picked up the sleeping girl, cradling her in his arms. "I want her more than I've ever wanted anything. My existence has lacked meaning till now."

In a quick step Navid crossed his path, halting Oviello's progress. "Then why, brother? Why send her away? She will bear us children, will she not?"

"That may be so but her will grows daily. Even now I sense the resistance of her mind. Infinitesimal as it might be, Bel's blood runs in her veins. The dreams will soon lose their potency."

"Wake her then."

Oviello walked past his brother and onto the nymphaeum where the sun bathed the marble in copper. Long shadows drifted across the colonnades. "Once a mortal wakes to our world they cannot return. She would be forever trapped."

"Is that not the point?"

The towering satyr paused. Oviello wanted nothing more than to keep the woman but keeping her would mean sharing her, keeping her as a captive or worse. Oviello wanted more. He had given all of his brothers a chance to breed but he had also lied to them. Oviello had broken a cardinal law of his people. He had bound the mortal to him without her consent. Once this was discovered his life would be forfeit.

"Navid," Oviello stated sternly, "do you not know the laws of our people?"

The younger man fell silent. Shoulders hunched, Navid frowned, seeking some answer that might dissuade his brother but no such answer existed. "Then that's it?"

Oviello nodded, slinging Gia over his shoulder. "Such is the Fates' will."

The two brothers locked gazes as the hint of a smile twisted the corners of their mouths. They clasped hands jovially, the tension between them dissipating.

"Females," scoffed Navid, "nothing but trouble. There will be others."

"Indeed. Feel free to leave my turn for last if you should come upon one!" chuckled Oviello, picking up his travel satchel.

"Be well, brother," smiled Navid, straightening. "I am headed back to the river to those damnable nymphs. One of them might yet be coerced to bear me some children!"

Oviello slung the pack over his free shoulder and smiled. "Good luck, little brother."

"It is you who will need the luck when I deliver the news of your poor decision to Naias and Arianno! Bel be with you!"

Gia did not stir or move as Oviello bounded down the steep hill, moving silently under the evening stars. In the distance, he could yet hear the mournful sound of Navid's aulos. His brother's tune was rooted in sadness, dating to the days when the veil was drawn between worlds, segregating mortals from Bel's bounty. It stirred the soul.

"Gia, honey, you with us?"

Startled, Gia nearly jumped in her chair. Her boss, a forty-something fashion veteran from Armani, leaned over the conference room table, his manicured eyebrows raised. It was always a sign of trouble when he cast that particular look and Gia had seen it way too many times since she had returned from her Italian vacation.

"Sorry, Carl." She cleared her throat and refocused on the PowerPoint presentation where dozens of Spring fashion trends were being reviewed. It was August and Janus Blake was lagging behind other designers for the Spring Collection.

"I think the plaid or the paisley should work. Maybe we go with olive, I think it would be really different if we paired it with coral for Spring. I have a few swatches I picked up from Surtex that I haven't seen on anyone's trend boards. We can really make a statement with a masculine pattern and a feminine accent color. If we make a decision by the end of the week we can send it to China for production and get digital swatches before September."

Carl brought one hand to rest under his chin as if he were pondering the meaning of life. Seconds ticked by in silence before the proclamation was made. "What do we think about plaid for Spring?"

The room buzzed for a moment as her coworkers immediately set to browsing the web for inspiration. It was a clever ruse to push the minute hand further towards lunch. It was nearly twelve thirty. Carl didn't have the fortitude to work through lunch and his new lover was making it harder and harder to stay past six. As far as she was concerned, the new flame deserved an award for tapering Carl's bitchiness.

As if on cue, Carl clapped his hands. "O.K., fashionistas, it seems Gia has given us food for thought. Get your badass selves to lunch and we'll resume at two-thirty. Chop-chop, off you go."

Distractedly, Gia closed her laptop and gathered her notes. The meeting had been a grueling affair that was likely to continue for the rest of the week. Trend decisions were never made lightly. Around her, the conference room vacated and she cursed herself for being the last one to pack up.

Carl glided to her side and gave her the eyebrow once more. "Everything O.K.?"

As bosses went Carl was better than most. Gia smiled, nodding. "Yeah, absolutely, didn't mean to space out before. I'll bring those samples with me when we get back."

Carl gave her a half smile. "You know I would never in a million years consider plaid for Spring but you haven't been wrong yet." The tall, thin man hesitated before continuing, "I have to ask, Gia, about what we discussed. Is your decision really final? I think Blake is gonna flip when he finds out. Anyway I thought you might reconsider. That offer is still on the table, girl. You're the golden goose of trends around here and I'd hate to lose you."

Gia slid the laptop into her backpack and leaned on the side of the mahogany table. Her decision to resign from Janus Blake and relocate to Italy had been made on pure impulse. "I'm not sure of anything right now, Carl, but I need a change. I think I'm done with New York for a while. Maybe when I settle I can be of some help remotely, keep on top of the Italian fashion scene from my farmhouse or something."

The man's eyebrows nearly connected at the mention of the word farm. "Gia, baby, I hope you think about this. In the meantime feel free to join us for lunch. We're headed out for sushi across the street."

"Thanks, Carl, I might join you in like ten. I have some phone calls I need to make."

With a smile Carl turned and swayed towards the door, pulling at his short, spiked hair. "See you soon."

Gia stared after him a moment, lost in the reflections of the mirrored conference-room doors. The woman in the mirror was not the same girl who had booked a trip to Italy a month prior hoping to get laid. She was not the same girl who fumbled over words and was shy around the opposite sex. The stranger in the mirror had fire in the eyes, a certain wildness that had never been there before.

Taking a deep breath, Gia gathered her things, shaking off the dark thoughts that crept into her mind, thoughts that seemed to consume her since her mysterious abduction. She had settled on abduction because it was the only thing that made sense. She couldn't account for the lost time or the series of broken memories that seemed to invade her every waking moment.

Since her return, Gia's days and nights had been filled with recollections of a man whose dark voice haunted her. The words, you are mine, tugged the deepest parts of her soul. It was a calling that was as powerful as it was enticing. It also filled her with dread.

Gia had awoken naked, five days later, in the very spot where she had lain down to rest in Hadrian's olive groves. She recalled vividly the faces of the men she had made love to with drunken wantonness and yet she couldn't be sure any of it was real. Her travel paranoia had served her well and she was grateful for the spare set of clothes she had packed in her backpack. It had saved her the embarrassment of having to trudge back to the tourist office in her birthday suit.

Immediately Gia had gone into work mode, making calls to her mother and her job, rescheduling flights and making up various stories about her late return. Carl had gotten the food poisoning story and her mom the one about branching off to Venice. She had managed the situation expertly except for the fact that she had no answers about what exactly had happened to her.

There were five days missing from her life that Gia could not account for. She recalled the wild, lustful faces, picnics in the countryside, gleaming mosaics, oil, wine being poured over her body and all kinds of things that made her blush. She still felt those amber eyes boring into her soul, the weight of Oviello's body pressed hotly against hers. The feel of their tongues, hands that caressed her without respite. Beneath the dark hair she had felt the curving horns; along his thighs, the fur.

It would have been easier to accept insanity than the prospect that she had been raped. For weeks after her trip she had grappled with the evidence. Her body showed all the signs of being sexually used and yet, there was enjoyment—intense and all-consuming.

"Fuck," she cursed out loud as her phone rang. She stared at the number a long time before letting it go to voicemail. She was entirely unprepared to hear the news.

Shadow and light passed over her as she walked along the charcoal hallway that connected the offices of Janus Blake. People passed her by, said hello and nodded, putting forth their fake smiles, but in the weeks since her return from Italy, Gia had changed too much for their small minds to grasp. The Giovanna Bruno who was timid and plump, soft and insecure was gone.

She wound through the corridors until she found the sanctuary of her office. Setting the bag down, Gia closed the door and locked it. She had no intention of eating lunch or being social. Slumping on the red leather couch she sighed, facing the blinking phone. Knowing she could not ignore the message, she brought it up to her ear and pressed play.

Just like Italians to turn water into wine, Gia thought, staring dumbfounded at the crowds that flocked to the ivy-covered fountain in the center of the piazza. A half-dozen men serviced hundreds of outstretched hands, filling plastic cups from spewing nozzles. Bodies clamored by her, all smelling of alcohol as cheesy Italian music blared loud enough to shatter the ancient masonry of the medieval homes.

Her neighbor's suggestion to come to *Sagra dell'Uva* in Marino had been a terrible idea. There she was, single with a bottle of Pellegrino in hand, surrounded by drunken lovers, singing and dancing old people and wine flowing an inch deep along the cobblestones.

The decision to move to Tivoli, in hindsight, had not been one of her brighter ideas. Gia had spent the better part of September unpacking boxes, hiring plumbers, masons, and all manner of help in a language she barely understood. It had been hellish. Even with her plundered 401K, grandma's old house made her crammed, shared apartment in New York City seem like paradise.

Gia was alone, jobless, halfway through her budget for repairs and had as of yet even begun to try to piece together what had happened to her. Since her arrival in Rome the dreams and memories of her abduction had magnified, blossoming into a perpetual obsession. The dark voice inside her and her changing desires had been enough to arouse such fits of rage Gia was sure she'd be institutionalized.

She had drowned her ripening sexuality and the maddening dreams in her toil, working day and night to restore *nonna's* ancient home. From gardening to spackling to carpentry, Gia had tackled it all and more, turning herself into a regular Rosie the Riveter. Her nails told the tale of a woman on the verge of a nervous breakdown. Her hair was a tumbled mess that she had termed the *jungle je ne sais quoi*—a do that would have had Carl screaming at the top of his lungs. "If you could see me now, darling," she said, taking a sip of water.

Gia had discarded the pencil skirts and editor pants for wrap dresses, shorts and t-shirts. The days of hot yoga, pedicures and Swedish massages seemed like distant fairy tales in a land far, far away. Simplicity ruled her waking hours and yet, in spite of the abject lunacy of her decision, there was also a sense of tranquility that had settled in her bones. Setting foot on Italian soil again had felt invariably right–like destiny.

Gia walked through the crowd and smiled. It was a far cry from Fifth Avenue. Slowly, she circled the fountain, her eyes resting on the marble figure. It was an image she had seen before, recreated in countless paintings and murals. Statuesque, naked with hands upraised, Dionysius offered his grape bounty to the sky. Beneath him, fat little cherubs with urns spilled his godly wine while lower still were his fur-haunched and horned children. Gia stared, perturbed, at the dilapidated statues. Half men, half goat, stone muscles flexed beneath the wine god, they held the basin aloft that brimmed with Marino's pride and joy.

Nervously, Gia looked around the ruddy-faced crowd, before fixing her gaze upon the fountain once more. Memories of her strange sexual encounter with Oviello rushed to the forefront of her mind. Recognition struck like lightning along with a sinking feeling–the kind people must feel when they realize they've gone mad. Gia tried to move but her legs refused to obey. Sudden heat welled between her thighs as her eyes traveled down to the statues' furry thighs. Her breath caught, only to be slowly released and finally swallowed hard.

People bumped into her but it was all a blur. Gia stood motionless for what seemed an eternity—lost in desire and the confusion of her jumbled thoughts. She heard her name called out but it sounded far away and muffled. It was not until a hard body pressed against her and hands traveled along her hips that she realized she was being groped.

Gia wanted to snap out of her reverie and lash out, scream, turn and defend herself but she was glued to the ground as the hands continued their slow ascent. The touch felt warm and enticing, igniting her desire. Her hunger for a man's touch had not been sated for months and in that moment she hated herself for enjoying it.

Behind her, Gia felt the distinct hardness of hips. The noise of the crowd dimmed, becoming a low pulse as whispered words in a strange language seized her senses.

Suddenly dizzy and jelly-kneed, Gia felt the world sway in the blaring heat of the sun until the piazza spun, becoming a blur of color. "Help," she heard herself whimper as darkness came.

"Thegasus mei non leinos." The gentle words pushed past her subconscious, slowly beginning to make sense. "Do not fear me." The gentle hands returned, soothing her sweaty brow. Gia opened her eyes, breathing in the smell of the sea. In the distance she could still hear the polkas of the festival, the cries of the crowd.

Her vision returned before solidifying on the figure who held her. Above her, the man of her dreams looked down, his amber eyes blazing into hers. Oviello held her in his arms, his hands soothing away her fears.

A million questions surfaced only to drown in the beauty of his face. Gia's heart ran, tripped and stumbled, kicking the insides of her chest so hard she thought she might die. She stared into the honey ocean of his eyes, allowing the burn in her blood to sing the inexplicable medley of feelings that wrestled in her soul. Relief, desire, anger, love, damnation, elation all screamed at once and all Gia could do was smile.

Oviello smiled back, his own eyes reflecting hers. Unable to speak, they held each other in the cool shadow of the ancient cypress and remained thus a long time. Hearts beating wildly, tears welling in their eyes, they pulled at each other.

"I hoped you might return to me," he said, kissing her wet cheeks, "I prayed to Bel that you might."

Gia clung to him, her hands seeking proof that he was truly real. "I was afraid. I didn't know what had happened to me. I went home. I couldn't be sure you were even real. I have these fragments of memories–"

Oviello pulled her into his arms until she was cradled upon his chest. "I was afraid to show you who I truly was. Afraid you wouldn't accept me."

Gia looked at him, searching for any evidence of the beast she was sure she had seen in the darkness of the cavern. "How did you find me?"

Oviello nuzzled into her neck, sucking in her fragrance and the smell of summer heat. "I can feel you, Gia, you are my mate. Our souls are tied. Don't let your eyes deceive you, this skin of man that I wear is but a clever ruse—an illusion. I am as you remember though I did my best to conceal it." His arms wrapped around her waist. "Times like these, when your people venerate my creator, Bel, our kind can wander into your world as men. *Sagra dell'Uva* is one of many such festivals. Though the religion of the bleeding man has tried to take it from us, Bel sways mortal hearts with wine. I found you by chance. When you returned I felt you near but I could not go to you. Today, this day, was my only chance and Gia, by Bel, I did my best to call to you."

Tears rose up. Gia tried to stifle them but it was no use. Emotion poured from her like wine from the fountains of Marino. She turned in his arms and wrapped herself around him. "I came to find you," she sobbed, her fist landing lightly on his shoulder. "I had no idea where to look. I had no name, no place, nothing to go on. I went back to the ruins, hoping, and found nothing."

Oviello kissed her, his loving hands caressing her back. "The ruins," he said quietly, "are no longer my home. After I released you I... had to make a choice. I either stayed with my brothers without you as my soulmate or sought you out. Without our bonded mates we *Satyroi* slowly grow wild and feral. It would have been an easy discovery that I had bound you once the madness set in. Either way it would have spelled death.

It was wrong to bind you against your will, Gia, forgive me."

"I do not fully comprehend everything you have said but those missing five days of my life have come to mean more than the rest. I love you."

"And I you," Oviello sighed, bringing her tear-streaked lips to his. "I need you," he gasped into her hungry mouth as passion overcame them. The kiss was as ferocious as it was tender. The two lovers cleaved to each other, their hands and lips seeking the comfort of the other. Fingers sought every crevice, hands any exposed skin as the succulent kiss became all the explanation they needed.

In the shade of a cypress they lay, tangled with each other, allowing their tongues to venerate the love they felt in their hearts. Oviello's hand pushed under her skirt, seeking his lover's warm, slippery thighs. Gia pulled at the loose cotton fabric of his shirt until her hungry palms found purchase on his hard body. It was a maddening and urgent dance as clothes were shed and torn.

Gripping her thighs, Oviello pulled her roughly against his hips, his eyes devouring the sight of her swollen breasts. "You are a goddess in the flesh," he murmured, positioning himself at the entrance of her slick heat.

"Wait," warned Gia, through clenched teeth, lust pounding in her ears.

"An eternity if I must," smiled Oviello, drawing her down to flick his tongue over a hard nipple.

"Is this real?"

Oviello bit her gently, his hands roaming over her belly. "Is this?"

Stunned, Gia eased back. "What?"

"Gia, there is no going back for me. I have forsaken my people and their vagrant, glorious paradise. I am here to stay and grow old with you. You carry my child. My place is at your side."

Wide-eyed, Gia stared down at him, her supple lips growing into a mischievous smile. Maybe coming to Italy wasn't such a bad idea after all.

THE END
~ for now ~

ABOUT NARCISSE NAVARRE

Narcisse Navarre was born in Habana, Cuba in 1975. She grew up surrounded by nature in a world nearly devoid of media. Prompted by her father's nightly tales of the Greek Gods, folklore and magic, Narcisse's imagination blossomed into an extraordinary force in her life.

In 1984 she emigrated to the United States where she was able to realize her dream of becoming an artist, poet and author. Spiritual, fiery and passionate, Narcisse is an avid world traveler and adventure seeker. Whether she is wreck diving, zipping through Belizian jungles or strolling through Roman ruins, Narcisse is always looking for way to incorporate her experiences into her writing.

Currently, Narcisse is co-authoring a trilogy of dark fantasy novels.

For more information visit:
Khajj.com, NarcisseNavarre.com, DigitalAlchemist.com

www.ingramcontent.com/pod-product-compliance
Lightning Source LLC
Chambersburg PA
CBHW020645130626
46552CB00003B/1413